SATOMI ICHIKAWA

Suzette and Nicholas
and the Sunijudi Circus

MICHÈLE LOCHAK
and
MARIE-FRANCE MANGIN
Translated by Joan Chevalier

THE SUNIJUDI CIRCUS

PHILOMEL BOOKS
New York

A circus had come to town!
Suzette and Nicholas and Benjamin
were so excited they couldn't keep still.

Nicholas had brought a letter home from school for his mother to read. In the letter, the teacher explained that the circus was a summer camp for children from many different countries. These children were learning to be real circus performers. They would practice every day and the school children from the village would practice with them.

"Please, Mommy, may we go?" asked Suzette. "Julie and Dillon can come too."

The answer was yes and soon the children stood in front of the large pink and white striped tent.

"I could never do that!" said Julie when she saw a boy standing on his hands.

"Oh, that's easy," said Suzette.

"We'll see about that!" answered Nicholas. He had heard his sister say things like this before.

The four friends ran to the narrow wooden barre. They sat on it, swung from it by their knees—and sometimes fell from it. Luckily, the ground was not very far below.

As Suzette climbed up the rope, she wondered how Natasha managed to go down a rope headfirst. She watched Alex swing from the trapeze by his knees. Below, a girl walked the tightrope. There was so much to learn from the circus children.

The children thought it was fun to
balance on a unicycle, a ball, or a pair of stilts.

Suzette tried tumbling but couldn't
seem to land on her feet.

Nicholas found that it wasn't
easy to go around in a circle while
turning cartwheels. He certainly
needed more practice.

Suzette learned to juggle while
Nicholas and Julie tossed rings
to each other. Somehow the rings
never went where they were
supposed to. They landed on
the ground instead.

The children learned how to act, too, because acting
is an important part of being in a circus.

Soon they were able to show how it felt to be
tired...

...and how it felt to be happy and full of energy.

Dance classes were given inside the house. The children practiced in front of a huge mirror.

"Hold on to the barre," said Natasha, "and listen to the music."

Suzette couldn't keep her leg straight and Nicholas kept leaning forward.

"Straighten your legs and flatten your backs!" said Natasha. "Let's begin again from the beginning. Arm forward, leg back…"

And so the days passed, working and having fun together. Then, one very special evening, the circus children gave a real performance. All the people from the village came. They made a very large audience. There was lots of excitement and laughter.

After the opening parade, the clowns and jugglers, acrobats, musicians and dancers, went backstage to wait for their turns to perform. Suzette and Nicholas and their friends were allowed to help. Their job was to put out mattresses so the acrobats would not be hurt if they fell.

The ringmaster announced the first act.

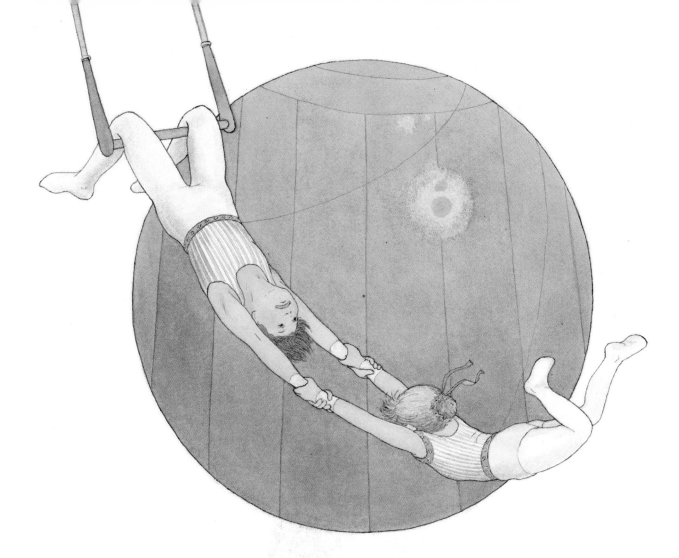

Spotlights danced on the ceiling of the tent.

"The flying trapeze is scary," said Suzette.

"Yes, but they've practiced very well," answered Nicholas. "Watch them...they look like birds."

"Yes, they look as if they're going to fly up to the top of the tent," said Suzette.

At the sound of drums the audience was quiet. The acrobats were going to try a double flip. Suzette held her breath, it was so exciting. They made it! Everyone clapped loudly.

Then spotlights lit up a graceful figure. A small Japanese girl holding a parasol danced lightly along the tightrope. Suzette and Julie loved this act, which looked so easy to do.

"If only I could do that," sighed Julie. She had tried to walk the tightrope and knew how hard it was.

The drums sounded again. This time, jugglers
appeared, tossing rings of every color. The children
were amazed to see that not a single ring was dropped.

Next came the brave horseback riders. They galloped around the ring, pulling a brightly painted wagon with a clown in it. Every time the clown stood up he would fall down, making everyone laugh.

Then three more clowns came out and tried to play some music. They made terrible noises, and the children laughed and clapped loudly.

The circus was over much too soon. The performers came out to take their final bows.

21

The next day Nicholas said, "Let's have a circus of our own!" Suzette, Julie, and Dillon all thought that was a good idea. They borrowed the costumes and other things they would need from the circus children and made a banner. They named the circus after themselves, using two letters from each of their names.

Dillon was the strong man. No one in the audience needed to know that he was really just lifting a broomstick with two balloons attached to it. Or that the plates Suzette was pretending so hard to balance were really fastened firmly to the sticks she held.

Then it was time for the animal trainer's act. Dressed as a clown, Nicholas held a hoop while Dudley jumped through it. But when it was Melissa's turn, things were different. She would not jump, but purred and wanted to be petted instead. Everyone laughed, even Nicholas.

Next there was a human pyramid, which made everyone clap loudly. Even Benjamin joined in the fun.

In the final act, Julie was a graceful windup
doll. Around and around she turned on
one foot.

Then Suzette played some music very loudly and very badly. All the children put their hands over their ears. Even Dudley covered *his* ears! But it was very funny and the Sunijudi Circus was a big success.

The summer went all too quickly. Soon it was over, and it was time for the circus children to leave the village. Suzette, Nicholas, Julie, and Dillon would miss them.

"Goodbye," they called as they waved to their new friends. "Be sure to come back next summer!"

Satomi Ichikawa was born and grew up in
Gifu, Japan. Since 1971 she has lived in Paris
but she also feels at home in England and the
United States, where she is a frequent visitor.
A very young artist, Satomi Ichikawa is already
emerging as one of the really important illus-
trators of children's books. Her exceptional
artistic talent lies in her ability to recreate the
world of childhood as it appeared in classic
children's book illustrations years ago and
yet, at the same time, to paint modern children
who are very much part of our world today.
She has illustrated many books for young
people, among them *Playtime*, *Under the
Cherry Tree*, and *Sun Through Small Leaves*.

PHILOMEL BOOKS
*are published by The Putnam Publishing Group
200 Madison Avenue, New York, N.Y. 10016*